LARK
Holds the Key

NATASHA DEEN
Illustrated by MARCUS CUTLER

orca Echoes

ORCA BOOK PUBLISHERS

Library and Archives Canada Cataloguing in Publication

Deen, Natasha, author
Lark holds the key / Natasha Deen ; illustrated by Marcus Cutler.
(Orca echoes)

Issued in print and electronic formats.
ISBN 978-1-4598-0727-3 (paperback).—ISBN 978-1-4598-1129-4 (pdf).—
ISBN 978-1-4598-1130-0 (epub)

I. Cutler, Marcus, illustrator II. Title. III. Series: Orca echoes
PS8607.E444L37 2016   jc813'.6   C2016-900540-2
                             C2016-900541-0

First published in the United States, 2016
Library of Congress Control Number: 2016931887

Summary: In this early chapter book, rookie detectives Lark Ba and her twin brother, Connor,
come to the rescue when the town librarian misplaces her library key.

Orca Book Publishers gratefully acknowledges the support for its publishing programs provided
by the following agencies: the Government of Canada, the Canada Council for the Arts and the
Province of British Columbia through the BC Arts Council and the Book Publishing Tax Credit.

Cover artwork and interior illustrations by Marcus Cutler
Author photo by Curtis Comeau

ORCA BOOK PUBLISHERS
orcabook.com

Printed and bound in Canada.

21 20 19 18 • 7 6 5 4

For Navin, Maya & Kiran.

Chapter One

My name is Lark Ba, and I have ants in my pants. Not really. That would be gross. And not so much fun for the ants. *Ants in my pants* means it's hard for me to sit quietly. It's something my *halmoni*—that's Korean for *grandmother*—says when I'm really ~~exsited~~ ~~exceted~~ excited. Only I wasn't sitting—I was lying down in bed. Waiting. Patient-like. Until...

"Psst. Connor." I leaned over and looked at the bottom bunk. "Connor, are you awake?" Connor's my *little* brother. He's *much* younger than me.

"Yes. I'm awake. Are you?"

I sighed. "Yes. If I was sleeping, I wouldn't be talking, would I?"

"Yes, you would. You talk a lot."

I ignored that. "Are you excited?"

"Yes. Today is going to be awesome."

"It's going to be the bestest day ever!"

"Lark, you say that every day. Anyway, *bestest* isn't a word."

I sighed. "It should be. It's a great word." I love words. Maybe I should be a writer when I grow up. Then I could make up great words like *bestest*. I turned on the lamp and said, "Yep. I'm gonna be a writer. Then I'm gonna make *bestest* a word."

"Lark, *gonna* isn't a word either. Anyway, I thought you were going to be an actor."

"I think I'll be both. That way, I can write the stories I want to act in."

Connor rolled his eyes.

I decided to be patient because he was just little. I climbed down from the top bunk. Today was the third day of summer vacation. On the first day, Connor and

I started a circus. We tried to teach our dog, Max, how to dance. He wasn't so good at that. And we broke two lamps. Mom said we had to do something else. Something that didn't include Max. Or her lamps.

Yesterday, we tried to do a people-only circus with our friends Kate and Franklin. No lamps were broken. But Franklin tried to do a special jump. He jumped great. But he also made a hole in the wall with his head. Dad said no more circuses. He used his grumpy voice. And that's when Halmoni suggested we all go to the library instead.

Only Halmoni didn't call it a library. She called it The Temple of Secrets. She said books contained secrets between their pages. And when you read a book, you could find all kinds of treasure!

"I'm going to get fifty books," I told Connor.

"I'm going to get a hundred. Do you think Mom and Dad will remember to take us?"

I nodded. "Yes. I put a note on the fridge. And in the bathroom. And in their shoes. And in their coat pockets." I would have put one in their car too. But *Babu*—that's Swahili for *grandfather*—told me a long time ago that I wasn't supposed to be in the car without a grown-up.

"Are you sure they won't forget?" Connor looked worried.

I knew because his forehead went all ~~skiggly sqwiggly~~ squiggly.

"What if they don't wake up in time?"

I sighed. Little brothers are so much work. "If you're worried, let's go check."

"I'm not worried, but the last time we woke them up—"

"I say we should go. It shows we have…" I couldn't remember the word. It started with an *n* or maybe an *i*, and it was a good word. "It shows we care. I'm your big sister, and that's my decision."

"You are not older!"

"Yes I am."

"We're twins!"

"I'm the older one."

He made a growly noise. "Only by ten minutes."

"Still older." I gave him my best big-sister look. "Are you going to come with me? Or are you too scared?"

Chapter Two

We went quiet-like to Mom and Dad's room.

Connor put his ear to the door. His face went all wrinkled. "Dad's snoring. I think they forgot about the library."

"Let's wake them."

He did a little walk backward.

What a fraidy-cat. But I'm a good big sister, so I didn't say anything. "There's nothing to be scared of." Okay, I almost didn't say anything. "Let's go." I pushed open the door and went inside. The blankets went up and down with Dad's snoring and Mom's breathing.

I went up real close to Dad. His eyes were shut tight. I leaned in to make sure. "Dad. Dad." I whispered softly because Halmoni said it wasn't nice to wake people up loudly. I tapped him on the forehead. He kept snoring.

Connor tugged on my shirt. "I don't know about this."

"It's fine." I tapped harder.

Dad kept snoring.

Now I was *really* worried. What if they didn't wake up? I didn't want to be late. Gentle-like, I put my finger on Dad's eyelid and lifted. "Dad?"

"Arrrgghhh!" he screamed.

"Aaaaahhhh!" Conner screamed.

"Aaaaaiieee!" Mom screamed the loudest and jumped out of bed.

"Lark!" Dad was using his grumpy voice. "What are you doing?"

"Making sure you're awake. We have to go to the library."

Mom looked real hard at the clock. Then she crawled back into the bed. "Honey, it's five in the morning. The library doesn't open until ten."

I did the math. "That's five hours away."

"Yes." Dad was back to using the Dad voice I liked. "Do you know what that means?"

I thought hard. "We have time for French toast?"

Chapter Three

Halmoni had heard the screaming. She took us from Mom and Dad's room to the kitchen.

"Can we have French toast?" I asked.

"If you help," she said.

Halmoni is Dad's mom. Babu is Mom's dad. If he had been here, he would have made us *uji*—that's porridge. But he was in Kenya, counting elephants. I'd wanted to go with him, but he'd said

I would scare the elephants. He laughed when he said it, so I knew he was joking.

I love Halmoni and Babu. They never use their grumpy voices with me. Or with Connor. That's amazing because he can be really ~~anoiing~~ ~~anoying~~ annoying. "I'll help make French toast."

"Me too," said Connor. He pulled a chair to the counter.

Halmoni gave me a piece of paper. "That's the recipe. You read it. Connor and I will do what it says."

"Did you hear that, Connor? You have to do what I say." I leaned in and whispered, "Because I'm older."

He did the growly voice thing.

"And get your special paper," called Halmoni.

I have *d-y-s-l-e-x-i-a*. Dyslexia. It means my brain works differently when

I have to read letters and numbers. I went to my school drawer and took out one of my see-through, colored pieces of paper. Then I put it on top of the white paper Halmoni gave me. It made the letters and numbers stop jumping on the page. And that made the words easier to read. I told Halmoni and Connor what to do. Pretty soon we had lots of yummy French toast.

Connor ate a bunch.

I only wanted two pieces. But they tasted really good, so then I had two more. "Maybe one more," I told Halmoni. "I didn't know I was such a good cook."

When we finished eating, we cleaned up. Then I double-checked that I had my library card. I checked for my cloth bag to carry home the books. And I triple-checked Connor's stuff. Soon we'd be at the library!

Chapter Four

Dad wanted to come with us, but he had to work at the ~~ahkarium~~ ~~akwairium~~ aquarium. So Halmoni, Mom, Connor, Max and I walked to the library. On the way to the library were the tailor's shop, the baseball field, the park and my favorite place—the ice-cream shop. I tried to tell Mom we should get some ice cream. She said it was too early.

"Besides, Lark, it's not even hot out yet!"

"But it will be," I told her. "And eating ahead is just good planning."

Mom made a weird sound in the back of her throat.

Halmoni got the coughs and turned her face away.

We kept walking. Soon I could see the roof of the library. It was one of the places I liked best! There were lots of windows and cozy places to sit. There was a fireplace in the library. In the winter, I loved sitting by it and reading my books.

"I'm going to get books on astronauts and the guys who get to study stars," said Connor.

"I'm going to get books on real detectives," I said.

"Detectives?" His face went scrunchy. "Why? I thought you wanted to be an actor or a writer."

"I do. I'm going to be a great actor and a great writer. And that means reading as many stories as I can. That way, I can learn everything about everything." I stopped. "Hmm, I kind of already know everything."

Connor snorted.

"But I'll know *more* of everything. It'll make me a great actor. And writer."

Connor nodded. "That's a good idea. I should probably get some books on fixing rocket ships too. I'm going to be the first person on Jupiter. I should know how to fix something if it breaks."

"See? It's good to have a big sister, isn't it? Aren't I a good teacher?"

He heaved a sigh and rolled his eyes. "Twins, Lark. We're twins."

I sighed too. Little brothers can be so much work. I decided to ignore him and think of the books I was going to get. Detective stories! I like them a lot because there's a problem to solve. I'm an excellent problem solver. I know because I solve Connor all the time, and he's a *huge* problem.

Plus, on the last day of school, Principal Robinson read us a story about a detective. In the book, the detective called himself a P.I., which means *private investigator*. I liked that name, even though it took me a long time to learn how to spell it.

My name would look great with initials. Lark Ba, P.I. *Pluser*, investigator sounds like alligator, and I like them a lot.

The P.I. did this cool thing where he talked but his lips didn't move. I could do that too. Almost. And *plusest*, he got to wear a cool trench coat and an even cooler hat. I look *great* in hats!

Principal Robinson said that detective stories were great because they were full of deeds of derring-do. I didn't know what that meant, but it sounded *amazing*. At dinner I told Mom and Dad I was going to do derring-dos. Dad said that would be a huge change because I'm usually full of derring-dont's.

All the grown-ups laughed, but I didn't get the joke. Still, I laughed so they didn't feel bad.

Goodness, all this thinking was making me hungry. And excited. I *really* wanted to get to the library. Like, *now*!

We turned the corner for the library and I saw the doors. I also saw something else. And I did not like it one bit. Nope. Nope. Nope.

Chapter Five

The librarian, Mrs. Robinson, was married to our school principal. Normally we found her busily shelving books or helping people at the checkout counter. Today she was sitting outside on one of the benches. Well, not really sitting. She looked like one of my birthday balloons when they start leaking. Mrs. Robinson saw us and gave a sad wave.

"Mrs. Robinson, what happened?" asked Connor. "How come the library isn't open?"

She sniffled. Then she snuffled. "I lost the key to the library!"

Holy crickets. This was pretty big. No wonder she sniffled and snuffled. Connor lost our house key one time. Dad used his *really* grumpy voice when he found out.

I climbed onto the seat next to her. "Don't worry, Mrs. Robinson. Connor loses stuff all the time—"

"Hey," said Connor. "So do you!" He turned to the librarian. "Lark's lost her mittens and her sweater. And one time, Mom said Lark had lost her mind." He scrunched his mouth. "But I'm not sure how she knew that."

Mom made a gurgling sound.

Halmoni coughed.

I glared at Connor. Then I gave Mrs. Robinson a smile. Smiling always makes people feel better. "When Connor lost his key it was okay because I had mine. Does anyone else have a key?"

She shook her head sadly. "No. Well, yes. Milly, the assistant librarian, has one," said Mrs. Robinson, "but she's on vacation."

"This doesn't seem like very good planning," I told her. "Next time, Milly should maybe give her key to someone else. Someone who's responsible and stuff." I thought about it. "She should give it to me. I never lose stuff."

Connor laughed.

"She should give it to us," I said. "We hardly ever lose stuff."

Connor smiled and nodded.

Mom put her hand on her forehead and looked at the sky.

Mrs. Robinson gave me a shaky smile. "I'll tell her that."

"What about Pete?" asked Mom. "Can't he help?"

Pete was a...I don't know the name. But he got to break into people's cars and houses. Plus, he never got arrested. Pluser, he got to drive in a really cool truck.

"I phoned," said Mrs. Robinson. "He's out at the Andersons' farm, putting new locks on the house. He could be gone until this afternoon."

Hmm. This was a big problem. The library couldn't stay closed for that long. People would be upset with Mrs. Robinson, and I didn't like that. She was a nice lady.

"When I lose something, I close my eyes. I try to remember what I was doing when I lost the thing I lost."

Mrs. Robinson smiled back. "That's a good idea, Lark. That's what I was doing when you arrived. But I just can't think of where I lost it."

"Maybe you should tell us where you've been," I said, "and we can help."

She nodded. "I decided to walk to work today because it was such a lovely day."

Mrs. Robinson started talking about the sunshine and the birds. Then she said something about cleaning. At least, I think she was talking about cleaning. She said something about waxing ~~nostalgick nostalcick~~ nostalgic. I didn't know what that meant, but both Mom and Halmoni nodded. So I did too.

Connor frowned and opened his mouth.

I elbowed him.

He pressed his lips together and nodded at Mrs. Robinson.

The librarian stopped talking about cleaning and started to talk about books. "I started this great book last night," she said. "It was hard to put down. I woke up early just so I could keep reading."

"I know how you feel," I said. "The last book Principal Robinson read us was a mystery. It was very exciting." I thought about what the P.I. would do. He'd want more information. In the book, he was always saying, "Just the facts, ma'am." So I did too. But nicely. "What happened next?"

"I left home," said Mrs. Robinson. "I had my book in one hand. I had the library key in the other. Plus, I had my purse."

I nodded.

"Go on," said Connor. "What happened next?"

"Well, it was such a nice day and I was so early, I stopped at the park. I sat on a bench and kept reading. I was at this very exciting part in the book when I heard yelling. I looked up. There was Sophie McCallister and her friends. They were trying to fly a kite."

"Fly a kite?" Connor's face went all ~~wrinkley rinkly~~ wrinkly.

"But there's no wind," I said.

Connor snorted. "Sophie's so full of hot air, she doesn't need wind."

I glared at him. "Maybe it was a special kind of kite," I said.

He shook his head. "I don't think so. Anyway, Sophie and her friends are always up to no good. I bet they were doing something they shouldn't."

Sophie did get into trouble an awful lot. She was in the same grade as Connor and me. Sophie spent a lot of time with the teachers. And the principal. And writing apology notes.

Mrs. Robinson thought about what Connor had said. "No, they were definitely trying to fly a kite."

"Why were they yelling?" I asked.

"Sophie and her friends were fighting about something. I went over to see why."

Connor and I waited to see what she would say next.

"You were right about the wind," Mrs. Robinson said to Connor. "There wasn't any, and that meant they couldn't fly their kite. Sophie thought one of them should take the kite, climb a tree and jump out of it," Mrs. Robinson continued.

"Maybe that would get it to fly. I stopped them right away. That was a dangerous idea. Someone could get hurt."

Mrs. Robinson let out a big sigh that made her shoulders go up and down. "By the time I was done, it was time to go to work. I walked here. That's when I realized I'd lost my key."

My heart was doing a pitter-patter. Mrs. Robinson's story was just like the one in the book our principal had read. There was a mystery to solve. There were clues to find. I, Lark Ba, was going to solve it! I was going to be a P.I.! Today really was going to be the *bestest* day ever!

Chapter Six

"Mrs. Robinson," I said, "you have a mystery on your hands, and I'm going to solve it."

Connor stepped on my toe.

"I mean—*we're* going to solve it."

"How do you plan on doing that?" asked Mom.

"First thing we need to do is go to the scene of the crime."

Connor yanked on my sleeve. "But there's no crime. There's only a missing key."

"I know that." Brothers. They're such work! "But all P.I.s say that to start a case."

"Oh." Connor nodded. "Okay."

"I can't go," said Mrs. Robinson. "I have to wait for the locksmith."

Yes! *Locksmith!* That was the word for what Pete did. He opened locked doors. Because it was his job, he never got arrested. That was a pretty great kind of job. Maybe I should be a locksmith when I grow up. Then I could open the lock on Connor's treasure chest. And I wouldn't get into trouble, because it was my job!

"We can wait here," said Mom. "If Pete arrives, I can phone you."

Mrs. Robinson nodded. "Okay. Lark, what's first?"

"We should start with your bag," I said. "Can we please look inside?"

Mrs. Robinson nodded. We took out her wallet, a pack of gum, a travel mug, a hairbrush and her phone. But there was no key.

"I must have dropped it while I was walking," said Mrs. Robinson. "I should've put it in my purse pocket."

She looked really upset, so I patted her hand. "It's okay. With me and Connor on the case, your key will be found. Promise."

"Lark," whispered Connor. "You shouldn't make promises you can't keep."

I knew he was right, but in the P.I. book, the detective had promised the king he'd find the treasure. He called it "upping the aunty."

"We have to find the key," I told Connor. "I have to get more detective books. And I have to find out what 'upping the aunty' means." Plus, I needed to know what happened if you upped the uncle.

We said goodbye to Mom and Halmoni. Mrs. Robinson headed toward the park, with Connor and I close behind.

I couldn't wait to solve this case!

Chapter Seven

We hadn't been walking long when Connor pulled me aside. "Lark, how are we actually going to find this key? The park is gigantic. Plus, Mrs. Robinson said she walked for fifteen minutes. That key could be anywhere!"

"Not anywhere," I said. "*Somewhere.* Mrs. Robinson didn't walk all over the place. We just have to follow the path she took."

As we walked, I kept my head down, looking for clues. I was glad the sun was out. Maybe its light would reflect off the key. I concentrated hard. Really hard. I looked and looked and kept my head down.

And I walked right into a tree.

Connor laughed.

"Crickets!" I rubbed the spot on my head. "That hurt!"

Mrs. Robinson checked the bump. "Didn't you hear me yelling to stop?"

"No," I said. "I was concentrating on finding the key."

"Maybe we shouldn't do this," she said.

Double crickets! I couldn't lose the case! "No, it's fine." I glared at Connor. "My brother will keep an eye on me."

He snorted. "With you, I better keep two!"

I decided I needed to ignore him
because we were on a case. And because
Mrs. Robinson was there. I pulled
Connor close. "Didn't you pay attention
when the principal was reading the story?
She's a client, and we have to be..."
I couldn't think of the word. It was a

good one though. It meant to be on your best behavior. "We have to do a good job," I said. "Maybe she'll tell other people, and we can get more cases."

"More cases?" His eyebrows went to his forehead. "We can't even handle this one!"

I heaved a sigh. Little brothers. "Just look for the key."

We followed Mrs. Robinson back to her house. She showed us where she had stopped and admired the birds. She pointed out where she had waved at the lady gardening. Connor and I retraced Mrs. Robinson's every move.

But no key.

The library was still closed. There was no word yet from Pete. Connor looked really unhappy with me. And I was kind of wishing I'd left the aunty alone.

Chapter Eight

We spent some time looking for clues at the park but didn't have any luck. Finally Mrs. Robinson suggested we go back to the library. We started walking. Well, not really walking. More like shuffling. We were almost at the library when I realized we'd missed something.

"Sophie!" I said.

"Sophie, what about her?" asked Mrs. Robinson.

"Well, we walked the path you walked, and we talked to the people you talked to. But not to Sophie. She's kind of like a clue, because she was there. She might know something." I looked around. "We need to find her and talk to her."

"Oh," said Mrs. Robinson. "Sophie's like an eyewitness."

I knew that word! It was from the detective book. It was the word the P.I. had used to describe someone who had seen the crime being committed. "Yes, exactly like that!"

"That's a great idea. You kids go ahead and do that," Mrs. Robinson said.

She smiled, but I could tell she wasn't really happy. Her smile made her mouth move, but it didn't make her eyes go all crinkly.

"I should stay and wait for Pete," she said.

Connor nodded. "That's a good idea."

We watched her walk over to Halmoni and Mom.

"That wasn't a good idea," I said. "We need her to help solve the case."

"She's worried," he answered, "and she helped as much as she could." He took a deep breath. "It's up to us to figure this out."

He was right. Ugh. I hate it when he's right.

Chapter Nine

Finding Sophie was harder than I thought. We checked for her at the splash park. No Sophie. Then we went to the skate park. I didn't see Sophie, but I did see Franklin.

"Hello, Franklin," I said, "We're looking for Sophie. Have you seen her?"

He shook his head. "Did you try the splash park?"

"Yes," said Connor.

"Hmm." Franklin tapped his chin. "What about the arcade?"

"We haven't checked there," I said. "Thanks!"

Connor and I sped to the arcade. It was hard to stay focused on our case. The arcade was full of amazing video games. Plus, it had these awesome colored lights that blinked on and off and turned everything they touched into a rainbow of colors!

"Do you see her?" I yelled so Connor could hear me above the music of the games.

He shook his head. "We should try the mini-golf place."

We did, but she wasn't there. "You know who would know where she is?" said Connor. "Her mom."

"That's a smart idea."

He smiled and looked proud.

When we got to Sophie's house, I rang the bell. Sophie's mom answered the door.

"Hello, Mrs. McCallister," I said. "Do you know where Sophie is? We'd like to talk to her."

"Oh, she's upstairs! Hold on. I'll get her." She left to get Sophie.

I turned to Connor. "Isn't it funny that we'd find her in the last place we looked?"

Connor shook his head. "Of course it's the last place we'd look. Once we found her, why would we keep looking?"

I sighed. Brothers.

Sophie came to the door. She squinted at us and folded her arms. "Baa baa Lark sheep. What do you want?"

"That's not funny," said Connor.

"It *is* kind of funny," I said. "Because our last name is Ba and that's the sound sheep make."

Connor shook his head. "No, it's not. She's not making a joke. She's making fun of you." Connor stared at Sophie. "That's not cool."

"It's fine," I said. It was. Sophie and I are BFFs—she just doesn't know it yet. That's okay. I'm patient. But right now, I couldn't worry about friendship. I had a case to solve. "We need your help."

"No." She started to close the door.

"Wait." I stuck my foot in the door. And it hurt. But I ignored it. "This is something you want to do."

"Why?"

"Mrs. Robinson lost the key to the library. It's your chance to help her."

"I don't want to help her."

"But if you help her, she'll tell Principal Robinson."

"So?"

"So maybe he'll be nicer to you the next time you get in trouble."

"Like when school starts?" she asked.

I nodded.

"That's years away—"

"Actually, it's just two months away," Connor said, but Sophie wasn't listening.

"—forever away," she said. "He'll forget by then. Go away. I have stuff to do."

This was not going well. She didn't want to help Mrs. Robinson. She didn't want to help herself. Then I realized how I could get her to help.

Chapter Ten

"Sophie," I said, "if you help us with this case, I'll help you fly your kite."

"There's no wind, sheep brain." She scowled. "And I know you won't climb a tree."

"You're right on both counts," I said, "but I have an idea that I know will work. I promise."

Connor threw his hands in the air. "Another promise? Lark, you can't do that!"

"I can keep this one." I looked at Sophie. "So will you help?"

She thought about it. "Okay. Fine." She turned and yelled into the house, "Ma! I'm going out with the sheep people."

Connor growled.

Sophie ignored him. "Where are we going?"

"To the park."

"We're going to the park, Ma!" She closed the front door and started down the steps.

"Wait," I said. "We need your kite."

"Don't we also need her friends?" asked Connor.

I shook my head. "You can pretend."

He sighed.

Sophie went back inside and got her kite. It was really pretty. The kite was shaped like a diamond. It was lavender and had a long red tail. "I got it from my *babushka* yesterday."

Connor frowned. "What's a *babushka*?"

"It's a Ukrainian word," said Sophie. "It means grandmother. It was nice of her to send it to me, and I really want to make it fly."

"We will," I said, "as soon as we're done helping Mrs. Robinson."

We walked to the park and found the spot where she had been. "What now?"

"Connor, go with her. Pretend you're flying the kite. Then Sophie, yell at him when he won't climb the tree."

Sophie grinned. "I get to yell at him? Why didn't you say that before?"

I watched.

Sophie started yelling.

Connor sighed.

I yelled too. "Where exactly was Mrs. Robinson?"

Sophie stopped. Thought. Then she pointed left. "She was sitting on the bench."

"What did she do? Can you remember?"

"She stopped reading and looked up. Then she closed her book, rushed over to us and said we couldn't climb the tree and jump out of it." Sophie looked at the tree. "I wish we could've. I think it would have made the kite fly."

"But your friend would've fallen," said Connor. "Mrs. Robinson was right. It was too dangerous."

Sophie scowled. "Connor, you can be such a...such a...grown-up."

Connor's face went red. "Take that back!"

"I won't!"

I pushed in between them. "No *real* fighting!" Ugh. No wonder the P.I. in the book had worked alone. "We have a case to solve."

"I'm done helping!" Sophie grabbed her kite and ran off.

"No! Wait!"

But she ignored me and kept running.

"We don't need her anyway," said Connor.

"'Cause we're going to solve it on our own?"

He shook his head. "Lark, I'm not sure we can solve this. I think the key

is just lost. I'm going to go back to the library and wait. Come on," he said. "Maybe Pete will let us help with the lock."

I shook my head. "You go ahead. I'm going to solve this mystery. I promised."

He kicked at the ground. "Okay. Okay. Maybe I should stay."

"I made the promise, not you. Plus, Pete might let you play with the truck lights."

Connor's eyes went dreamy. "That would be a lot of fun."

I faked a smile and watched him go. As soon as he couldn't see me anymore, I let my smile fall away. Mrs. Robinson was gone. Sophie was gone. Connor was gone. And no one thought I could find the key. My bestest day ever had officially turned into my worstest day ever.

Chapter Eleven

I sat under the tree and thought. And thought. And thought some more. My head was starting to hurt from all the thinking. And I was getting hungry. I wished I'd eaten more of Halmoni's French toast. Something about this case just didn't quite add up. Something was missing.

Mrs. Robinson was a grown-up, and she was really, really responsible.

Maybe she really had just lost the key. But I didn't think so. And I didn't want to give up. And I *really* didn't want to break my promise.

I closed my eyes and listened to the wind in the trees. That made me feel better. But it didn't solve the problem. So I thought about what we had done so far. We had listened to Mrs. Robinson's story. Then we had followed her—as the P.I. would say, we had retraced her steps. Then we had listened to Sophie's ~~vershun~~ ~~verzun~~ version of the story.

What hadn't we done?

I listened to the wind again. Suddenly I realized what we'd missed. And that made me smile.

Chapter Twelve

I'd listened to Mrs. Robinson's story. I'd retraced the path she took to the library. But I, Lark Ba, who wanted to be an actor when I grew up, hadn't actually *pretended to be* Mrs. Robinson. Pretending to be someone is *way* different than just listening to their story. You have to feel what they feel, think what they think. That's called putting yourself in someone else's shoes.

I ran back to Mrs. Robinson's house. I pretended I had my book in one hand, my purse on my shoulder and the key in my other hand.

Then I started walking. I stopped and looked at the sky. I admired the birds. I thought about cleaning and waxing nostalgic. Then I kept walking. I got to the park, opened my book and pretended to hear Sophie fighting. I felt scared for Sophie and her friends. So I rushed to where they were. And I talked to the imaginary kids. Then I walked to the library.

And I looked down at my hand.

My imaginary key was gone.

But I was smiling.

Because I knew where it was.

Chapter Thirteen

"Mrs. Robinson! Mrs. Robinson!" I ran up to the librarian. "I know where your key is!"

"Where is it?" asked my mom.

"You found my key?"

"Great job, Lark!" said Halmoni.

"May I please see your book?"

Mrs. Robinson handed it to me.

I opened it. And there, placed in between the last two pages she'd read, was the key. "When you saw Sophie, you were worried and scared for her. And you weren't thinking of your key. You stuck it in your book so your hand would be free in case they needed you!" I stopped and thought. "And maybe so you didn't lose your place in the book too. That can be kind of annoying when it happens."

"Lark! You're amazing! Thank you!" Mrs. Robinson gave me a big hug.

And I hugged Connor. "Thanks for your help."

He didn't look happy. "I don't think I was really helpful. I'm sorry I left you."

"No, it was good you did. I got to be alone to think."

"Really?"

"Really, really."

He smiled. "Maybe I should leave you alone more often."

"I wish!"

Mrs. Robinson opened the library and everyone went inside.

Except me.

I still had one job to do before the case was over.

Chapter Fourteen

"Why are you here?" Sophie peered at me through the crack in the door.

"I told you I would help you fly the kite, and I will."

"Oh." She opened the door wider. "Did you solve your case?"

"Yes, I helped Mrs. Robinson. Now I can help you."

"But I didn't stay."

"You helped enough, and I made a promise. So are we going to fly the kite?"

Sophie watched me for a second. "Okay."

"Good. Just one thing first. I have to go to the library and get some books. And we'll need some grown-up help to fly the kite."

"The library?"

I nodded. "I want to get some books on detective work. I think I'm becoming a really good P.I. You want to come with me?"

Sophie shrugged. "Whatever. As long as you help me fly the kite."

We went to the library, and I got a bunch of mystery books. There were books on figuring out clues in dirt and how to find fingerprints. I got them too.

Then I helped Sophie find some books on kite repair—in case the kite got broken.

Halmoni and Connor came to Sophie's with us to fly the kite. Solving Sophie's problem was easy. She couldn't fly the kite because there was no wind. So we just had to make some. With the adult's help, we brought some fans outside and plugged them in. Then we turned them on. Now Sophie had the wind she needed to fly her kite!

And I'd fixed her problem. That was kind of like solving *two* cases in *one day*. I really was an amazing P.I.

Sophie looked at me. "Thanks, Lark sheep."

I smiled. "You're welcome."

Connor watched the kite sail in the sky. "That was a good idea."

"I know. I'm an excellent problem solver." I picked up my bag of books. "Get your books. We have to go."

"Where?" asked Connor.

"We solved Mrs. Robinson's problem. We solved Sophie's problem. I bet there are more mysteries and problems to solve. We need to find them."

Connor thought for a minute. "Okay, and next time, I won't leave you to play with truck lights."

"Good work today, you two," said Halmoni. "You helped out Mrs. Robinson and Sophie. That was kind of you."

"It was fun," said Connor. "I hope we get to help out more people this summer."

I agreed.

"You know what else would be fun?" asked Halmoni.

"What?" I asked.

"If we went to the ice-cream shop and each got a double scoop of ice cream."

"A double scoop?" Connor's eyes went bright and wide. "Are you kidding me?"

Halmoni smiled. "I think it could be just what a pair of detectives need to celebrate a job well done."

"I agree!" I said. "Let's get some ice cream!" Today *really was* the bestest day ever.

THE WORDS LARK LOVES

CHAPTER ONE:

*"I say we should go. It shows we have…"
I couldn't remember the word. It started
with an* n *or maybe an* i, *and it was a
good word. "It shows we care. I'm your
big sister and that's my decision."*

The word Lark was thinking of was
initiative. It's a great word! It means you
take charge of stuff. For example, if you
were finished eating dinner, taking the
initiative might be helping your parents
clear the table (without them asking)!

CHAPTER SEVEN:

"Didn't you pay attention when the principal was reading the story? She's a client, and we have to be..." I couldn't think of the word. It was a good one though. It meant to be on your best behavior.

Lark knew the definition but not the word. The awesome word she was thinking of was *professional*. For example, being professional in class could be making sure you're paying attention when your teacher or another student is talking.

THE STUFF LARK *ALMOST* GOT RIGHT

CHAPTER FIVE:

Mrs. Robinson started talking about the sunshine and the birds. Then she said something about cleaning. At least,

I think she was talking about cleaning. She said something about waxing ~~nostalgick nostalcick~~ *nostalgic. I didn't know what that meant, but both Mom and Halmoni nodded. So I did too.*

Waxing nostalgic is an old-fashioned way of saying you're thinking about the past and remembering fun memories. For example, when grown-ups talk about the toys they used to play with or the candy they used to eat when they were children, they're waxing nostalgic.

CHAPTER SIX:

I knew he was right, but in the P.I. book, the detective had promised the king he'd find the treasure. He called it "upping the aunty."

"We have to find the key," I told Connor. "I have to get more detective

73

books. And I have to find out what 'upping the aunty' means."

Lark thought the phrase was upping the *aunty*, but it's actually upping the *ante*. To up the ante means to ask more of yourself or others in order to complete a goal. For example, if you were playing baseball and could hit the ball five times in a row, upping the ante could be challenging yourself to see if you could hit the ball six times in a row.